# A THIRD
# CALDECOTT COLLECTION

*Illustrated by Randolph Caldecott:*

A FIRST CALDECOTT COLLECTION
The House that Jack Built • A Frog He Would a-Wooing Go

A SECOND CALDECOTT COLLECTION
Sing a Song for Sixpence • The Three Jovial Huntsmen

A THIRD CALDECOTT COLLECTION
The Queen of Hearts • The Farmer's Boy

*Illustrated by L. Leslie Brooke:*

JOHNNY CROW'S GARDEN
JOHNNY CROW'S PARTY
JOHNNY CROW'S NEW GARDEN

# A THIRD CALDECOTT COLLECTION

### THE QUEEN OF HEARTS
### THE FARMER'S BOY

## Illustrated by
## *RANDOLPH CALDECOTT*

FREDERICK WARNE

FREDERICK WARNE

Penguin Books Ltd, Harmondsworth, Middlesex, England
Viking Penguin Inc., 40 West 23rd Street, New York, New York 10010, U.S.A.
Penguin Books Australia Ltd, Ringwood, Victoria, Australia
Penguin Books Canada Limited, 2801 John Street, Markham, Ontario, Canada L3R 1B4

This edition first published 1986

ISBN 0 7232 3434 5

Typeset by CCC, printed and bound in Great Britain by
William Clowes Limited, Beccles and London

# The Queen of Hearts

R. CALDECOTT'S PICTURE BOOKS

# THE Queen of Hearts,

She made some Tarts,

All on a Summer's Day:

The Knave of Hearts,

He stole those Tarts,

And took them right away.

The King of Hearts,

Called for those Tarts,

And beat the Knave full sore :

The Knave of Hearts
Brought back those Tarts

And vowed he'd steal no more.

THE FARMER'S BOY

R. CALDECOTT'S
PICTURE BOOKS

WHEN I was a farmer, a Farmer's Boy,
    I used to keep my master's HORSES,
With a GEE-WO here, and a GEE-WO there,
    And here a GEE, and there a GEE,
    And everywhere a GEE;
Says I,    My pretty lass, will you come to the banks
    of the Aire oh?

When I was a farmer, a Farmer's Boy,
    I used to keep my master's LAMBS,
With a BAA-BAA here, and a BAA-BAA there,
    And here a BAA, and there a BAA,
    And everywhere a BAA;
With a GEE-WO here, and a GEE-WO there,
    And here a GEE, and there a GEE,
    And everywhere a GEE;
Says I,     My pretty lass, will you come to the banks
        of the Aire oh?

When I was a farmer, a Farmer's Boy,
    I used to keep my master's HENS,
With a CHUCK-CHUCK here, and a CHUCK-
        CHUCK there,
    And here a CHUCK, and there a CHUCK,
    And everywhere a CHUCK;
With a BAA-BAA here, and a BAA-BAA there,
    And here a BAA, and there a BAA,
    And everywhere a BAA;
With a GEE-WO here, and a GEE-WO there,
      &c.,    &c.,    &c.
Says I,    My pretty lass, will you come to the banks
        of the Aire oh?

When I was a farmer, a Farmer's Boy,
    I used to keep my master's PIGS,
With a GRUNT-GRUNT here, and a GRUNT-
        GRUNT there,
    And here a GRUNT, and there a GRUNT,
    And everywhere a GRUNT;
With a CHUCK-CHUCK here, and a CHUCK-
        CHUCK there,
    And here a CHUCK, and there a CHUCK,
    And everywhere a CHUCK;
With a BAA-BAA here, and a BAA-BAA there,
     &c.,     &c.,     &c.
With a GEE-WO here, and a GEE-WO there,
     &c.,     &c.,     &c.
Says I,    My pretty lass, will you come to the banks
        of the Aire oh?

When I was a farmer, a Farmer's Boy,
    I used to keep my master's DUCKS,
With a QUACK-QUACK here, and a QUACK-
        QUACK there,
      And here a QUACK, and there a QUACK,
      And everywhere a QUACK;
With a GRUNT-GRUNT here, and a GRUNT-
        GRUNT there,
        &c.,    &c.,    &c.
With a CHUCK-CHUCK here, &c.
With a BAA-BAA here, &c.
With a GEE-WO here, &c.
Says I,    My pretty lass, will you come to the banks
        of the Aire oh?

When I was a farmer, a Farmer's Boy,
　　I used to keep my master's DOGS,
With a BOW-BOW here, and a BOW-WOW
　　　there,
　　　And here a BOW, and there a WOW,
　　　And everywhere a WOW;
With a QUACK-QUACK here, and a QUACK-
　　　QUACK there,
　　　　&c.,　　&c.,　　&c.
With a GRUNT-GRUNT here, &c.
With a CHUCK-CHUCK here, &c.
With a BAA-BAA here, &c.
With a GEE-WO here, &c.
Says I,　My pretty lass, will you come to the banks
　　　of the Aire oh?

When I was a farmer, a Farmer's Boy,
    I used to keep my master's CHILDREN,
With a SHOUTING here, and a POUTING there,
    And here a SHOUT, and there a POUT,
    And everywhere a SHOUT;
With a BOW-BOW here, and a BOW-WOW
      there,
     &c.,     &c.,     &c.
With a QUACK-QUACK here, &c.
With a GRUNT-GRUNT here, &c.
With a CHUCK-CHUCK here, &c.
With a BAA-BAA here, &c.
With a GEE-WO here, &c.
Says I,    My pretty lass, will you come to the banks
      of the Aire oh?

When I was a farmer, a Farmer's Boy,
  I used to keep my master's TURKEYS,
With a GOBBLE-GOBBLE here, and a GOBBLE-
    GOBBLE there,
  And here a GOBBLE, and there a GOBBLE;
  And everywhere a GOBBLE;
With a SHOUTING here, and a POUTING there,
    &c.,    &c.,    &c.
With a BOW-WOW here, &c.
With a QUACK-QUACK here, &c.
With a GRUNT-GRUNT here, &c.
With a CHUCK-CHUCK here, &c.
With a BAA-BAA here, &c.
With a GEE-WO here, &c.
Says I,    My pretty lass, will you come to the banks
    of the Aire oh?